sky
rat

that
pesky
rat

lauren child

ORCHARD BOOKS

Thank you
Randala
and Albena

Look out for Lauren Child's
Clarice Bean books
and the award-winning
I will not ever
NEVER
eat a tomato

Max

and for anyone who
has ever wished they
were somebody's pet

Sam

Louie

Lucy

Zaida

and for fabulous
Frances and her
pets Lucy, Sam,
Ata and Cui

This book is for
the gorgeous Max
and her little
dog Louie

Sita

Flame

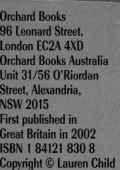

Twinkle

with love to Jo and Thomas,
long-suffering owners of Twinkle,
the Bette Davis of cats

Ata & Cui

Cheeky

Donut

Orchard Books
96 Leonard Street,
London EC2A 4XD
Orchard Books Australia
Unit 31/56 O'Riordan
Street, Alexandria,
NSW 2015
First published in
Great Britain in 2002
ISBN 1 84121 830 8
Copyright © Lauren Child
2002

The right of Lauren Child to be identified
as the author and illustrator of this work has
been asserted by her in accordance with the
Copyright, Designs and Patents Act, 1988.
A CIP catalogue record for this book is
available from the British Library
10 9 8 7 6 5 4 3 2
Printed in Singapore

This is me.
I'm the one with the **pointy** nose and **b e a d y** eyes.
The cutesy one
in the middle.

I live in dustbin number **3**, **Grubby** Alley.

Every now and again I come back to find someone has emptied **all my belongings** into a **big** van and driven off with them.
It's very **upsetting.**

I'm a brown rat, a street rat.
But people call me that pesky rat.
I don't know why.
They say I smell,
but that's not my fault, it's the dirt.

Sometimes when I am tucked into
my crisp packet,
I look up at all the cosy windows
and wonder what it would be like
to live with creature comforts.
To belong to somebody.
To be an actual pet.

Most of all I would like

to have a **name**, instead of just *that* **pesky** *rat.*

My friend Pierre, who is a **chinchilla**, is looked after by a rich lady called Madame Fifi. He has a very **glamorous** life.

He lives in the lap of **luxury**.

I say,

"I would quite like to live in a fashionable apartment and be fed chocolates while I sit on a feather cushion."

I hate having baths.

I think I'm **allergic** to soap.

Then there's this **Siamese** cat called **Oscar**. He lives with **Mr Washington**, a **busy** businessman.

Mr Washington is **always** at work so he doesn't have time to **wash fur** or be **strict**.

I'm quite good in the kitchen

but I hate

to be

bored.

Swinging on the trapeze one minute, tip-toeing on the high wire the next.

Nibbles says,

"It is fun hopping through hoops in a tutu. But sometimes I could do with taking off the clown's nose and putting my feet up."

You were divine darling!

Maybe it's all a bit nerve wracking for me.

I think I'd quite like one of those owners
who do lots of **sitting about**
like **Miss StClair**.

Her **Scottie dog, Andrew**, is **always** sitting by the

fire, having **supper** on a tray and they spend the evenings doing Puzzles together.

Andrew says,

"On the whole I feel **very well** looked after.

And **Miss StClair** is good company.

But it's rather **embarrassing** when we go out shopping."

Miss StClair makes Andrew wear a little hat and coat.

I don't think **clothes** would suit **me.**

But I would do **anything** to be somebody's **pet.**

So in the morning
I go to the pet shop
and ask Mrs Trill

if she has

an owner

who might want me.

She says,

"There isn't much call for brown rats,  and I'm afraid you aren't very **popular** with the public."

I say,

"I don't see why **not**. I'm very good **company**, always **popping up** when you least expect me to, and I am happy to eat **anything**, even if it's been slightly **nibbled**."

Mrs Trill says,

"Well, you could always make a **notice** and put it in the **window**. You never know."

So I write:

Me

Brown cat looking for kindly owner
with an interest in cheese
Hobbies include nibbling and chewing
would like a collar with my name on

would like a name
would prefer no baths
will wear a jumper if pushed
Yours keenly
            Brown cat (that pesky cat)

P.S sorry about bad paw writing

not
a very good picture

Then I wait **and** I **wait**

and   I   wait.   Until . . .

. . . on **Tuesday** old **Mr Fortesque** is passing
and he **stops** to look at my **notice**.

He has to really **squint** because he
has such **bad** eyesight.

Then he looks at me and says,

"**My,**
haven't you
got a pointy nose
and, goodness me,
what a long tail, and such
unusual beady eyes . . .

I'll take him."

I can't
believe my **luck,**
nor can Mrs Trill.

Mrs Trill says,
"Are you sure?"

And Mr Fortesque says,
"Oh yes, I've been looking for a brown cat
as nice as this one for ages."

Mrs Trill looks at me and I look at Mrs Trill,
and we both look at my notice,

but neither of us
says a word.

I just **love** being a **pet.**

And . . . I am trying to be **really** helpful.

I pick out the best **cheeses**

by using my excellent **sniffing** nose.

I clean the kitchen

by n i b b l i n g

up the

c r u m b s.

I help Mr Fortesque

I cross the road by **scaring** the traffic.

And I'm **always** there when he comes **home**.

So here I am.

Finally a pet with a name.

So what
if I have to
wear a little
jumper?

Mr Fortesque says, "Well, Tiddles, who's a pretty kittycat?"

And I squeak, "I am!"

that
pes